Babyberry Pie

Heather Vogel Frederick   illustrated by Amy Schwartz

HARCOURT CHILDREN'S BOOKS

Houghton Mifflin Harcourt

Boston   New York   2010

Text copyright © 2010 by Heather Vogel Frederick
Illustrations copyright © 2010 by Amy Schwartz

Harcourt Children's Books is an imprint of Houghton Mifflin Harcourt Publishing Company.

www.hmhbooks.com

The illustrations in this book were done in gouache and pen-and-ink on Rives BFK paper.
The text type was set in 20-point Pastonchi.   The display type was set in Caslon Open.
Designed by Christine Kettner

LIBRARY OF CONGRESS CATALOGING-IN-PUBLICATION DATA
Frederick, Heather Vogel.
Babyberry pie / Heather Vogel Frederick ; [illustrations by] Amy Schwartz.
p. cm.

Summary: In illustrations and rhyming text, gives the recipe for making "babyberry pie," from picking a baby
from the babyberry tree and popping him in the tub to putting powdered sugar on his nose and toes and
tucking him into pie crust covers.

ISBN 978-0-15-205927-9 (hardcover : alk. paper) [1. Stories in rhyme. 2. Babies—Fiction.
3. Bedtime—Fiction. 4. Humorous stories.] I. Schwartz, Amy, ill. II. Title.
PZ8.3.F869Bab 2010   [E]—dc22   2009036674
Manufactured in China   LEO 10 9 8 7 6 5 4 3 2 1
4500226431

For Babyberry Violet—H.V.F.

When the moon goes dancing
Across the starry sky,

It's time to bring the baby in
For babyberry pie!

First you pick a baby
From the babyberry tree—
One who's sweet,
A cuddly treat—
And bring him home to me.

Now it's time to wash him.

Let's pop him in the tub.

Scrub his toes,

His ears and nose,

With a kiss and a rub-a-dub-dub!

Babyberry's laughing!

He's having so much fun!

Splish-a-splash—

He makes a dash,

And now he's on the run!

Chase that little sillyberry, messyberry one!

Catch that little giggleberry, wiggleberry one!

Back into the bathtub.
Wash him fresh and clean.

Powder him from head to toe

And places in between.

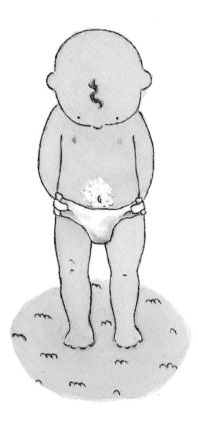

Sugar for his bellybutton!

Sugar for his nose!

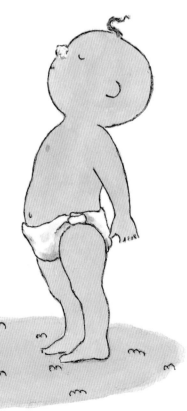

Sugar for his fingertips!

And sugar for his toes!

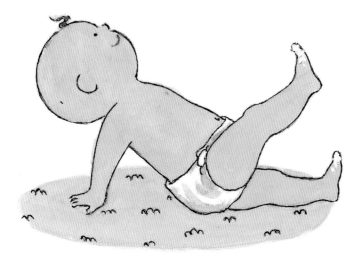

Next we make a pie crust—
Pile quilts and pillows high.

It's time to tuck the baby in
For babyberry pie!
Pop him in the pie crust.
Pull the covers tight.

Kiss the pie,
Wave goodbye,
And turn out all the lights.

For when the moon goes dancing

Across the starry sky,

It's time for pies

To close their eyes

And dream a lullaby.